Sam's No Dummy, Farmer Goff

by Brian Schatell

J.B. Lippincott | New York

Sam's No Dummy, Farmer Goff
Copyright © 1984 by Brian Schatell
Printed in the U.S.A. All rights reserved.

Library of Congress Cataloging in Publication Data
Schatell, Brian.
Sam's no dummy, Farmer Goff.

Summary: A turkey who can imitate the sounds of
other animals angers his farmer/owner by refusing to
make the sounds on a television show.
[1. Turkeys—Fiction. 2. Animal sounds—Fiction]
I. Title.
PZ7.S336Sam 1984   [E]   83-47669
ISBN 0-397-32061-2
ISBN 0-397-32062-0 (lib. bdg.)

First Edition
1 2 3 4 5 6 7 8 9 10

Farmer Goff lived on a farm with his wife and his prize-winning turkey, Sam.

Very, very early one morning, Farmer Goff was awakened from his sleep by the sound of a loud "Mooo!"
"Oh, no," yawned Farmer Goff, "my cow needs to be milked? It's only three o'clock in the morning."

MOOOOOOO

Nevertheless, he put on his slippers and went down to the barn.

But when he got there, the cow was fast asleep.
"What in tarnation?!" yelled Farmer Goff.
Just then he heard another loud "Mooo."

He ran outside, and there was Sam.
"Moooo!" said Sam.
"Why, you darn turkey!" yelled Farmer Goff. "You woke me up in the middle of the night!"

MOOO

Sam jumped up onto Farmer Goff's hat and said, "Baaaa. Baaaa."
"Get down, you crazy turkey!!" said Farmer Goff, waving his pitchfork wildly.

"Meeow!" answered Sam as he flew onto a fence, leaving feathers flying in Farmer Goff's face.

"That does it!!! I'll eat you for Thanksgiving dinner!!!" screamed Farmer Goff, and he lunged at Sam, pitchfork raised.

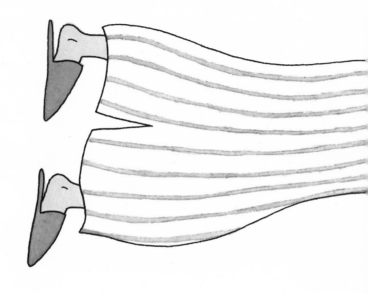

"Oink," Sam said, and he held out a poster:

WANTED! ANIMAL ACTS
FOR BIG-TIME TV SHOW!

Farmer Goff froze in midair.

"Turkeys don't say 'Mooo,'" he said. "They don't say 'Oink' either! We can go on that TV show with your act and I'll be famous!"

The next day Farmer Goff and Sam got into his truck and drove to the TV studio.

When they arrived, they found they were not the only animal act there. They picked a number and sat down next to a herd of performing cows.

Just before it was their turn to go on TV, Farmer Goff thought to himself, "Why should this dumb turkey get all the credit?" So he whispered to Sam, "Nobody will believe a dumb turkey can make all those sounds. So we'll pretend I'm a ventriloquist and you're my dummy!"

This made Sam mad.

"*I'm* the one who makes those animal sounds!" he thought to himself. "I'm nobody's dummy!"

Farmer Goff and Sam went onstage, said hello to the host, and sat down.

"What is *your* act?" asked the host.

"This is a ventriloquist act," said Farmer Goff, and he put Sam on his knee.

"Tell me, Sam," said Farmer Goff, "what is it that pigs say?"
But Sam made no noise.

"Well then, Sam," Farmer Goff said nervously, "what do cows say?"
Sam looked at Farmer Goff but remained silent.
The host and the audience started to snicker.

"Come on, Sam," said Farmer Goff, getting embarrassed and angry at the same time. "You know what pigs say—Oink! You know what sheep say—Baaa! And you know what cows say!" he yelled. "Moo! Go on and say 'Moo.' Moooo!!" he screamed. "Mooo Mooo Mooo MOOOOO!!!"

Suddenly there was a rumble from backstage, and to everybody's surprise, the herd of performing cows started stampeding wildly across the stage, followed by all the other animals.

The audience ran for their lives.

"Look what you made me do, you dumb turkey!" screamed Farmer Goff, jumping up and down. "You made a fool of me on TV! It's Thanksgiving dinner for you!"

But Sam was swept away by the herd and quickly disappeared out the studio door.

EXIT

In a minute Farmer Goff was swept along himself.

It was a bumpy ride.

In horror, Farmer Goff noticed that the animals were stampeding right toward his truck.

"Why you dumb turkey!" yelled Farmer Goff. "Stop them! Say MOOOO! Can't you say *anything*??"

"Don't look at me," Sam thought angrily. "I'm just a dumb turkey!"
And he jumped up, put his wings in his ears, rolled his eyes, stuck out
his tongue, and said:

"GOBBLE GOBBLE GOBBLE!!!"

Suddenly the stampede ground to a halt inches from Farmer Goff's truck...